A Note to Parents and Teachers

Kids can imagine, kids can laugh and kids can learn to read with this exciting new series of first readers. Each book in the Kids Can Read series has been especially written, illustrated and designed for beginning readers. Humorous, easy-to-read stories, appealing characters, and engaging illustrations make for books that kids will want to read over and over again.

To make selecting a book easy for kids, parents and teachers, the Kids Can Read series offers three levels based on different reading abilities:

Level 1: Kids Can Start to Read

Short stories, simple sentences, easy vocabulary, lots of repetition and visual clues for kids just beginning to read.

Level 2: Kids Can Read with Help

Longer stories, varied sentences, increased vocabulary, some repetition and visual clues for kids who have some reading skills, but may need a little help.

Level 3: Kids Can Read Alone

Longer, more complex stories and sentences, more challenging vocabulary, language play, minimal repetition and visual clues for kids who are reading by themselves.

With the Kids Can Read series, kids can enter a new and exciting world of reading!

Franklin and the Magic Show

From an episode of the animated TV series *Franklin,*
produced by Nelvana Limited, Neurones France s.a.r.l. and
Neurones Luxembourg S.A., based on the Franklin books
by Paulette Bourgeois and Brenda Clark.

Story written by Sharon Jennings.

Illustrated by Sean Jeffrey, Alice Sinkner and Shelley Southern.

Based on the TV episode *Franklin the Fabulous,* written
by Paula Butorac.

Kids Can Read is a trademark of Kids Can Press Ltd.

Franklin is a trademark of Kids Can Press Ltd.
The character Franklin was created by Paulette Bourgeois and Brenda Clark.
Text © 2002 Contextx Inc.
Illustrations © 2002 Brenda Clark Illustrator Inc.

Kids Can Press acknowledges the financial support of the Ontario Arts Council,
the Canada Council for the Arts and the Government of Canada, through the
BPIDP, for our publishing activity.

Published in Canada by
Kids Can Press Ltd.
29 Birch Avenue
Toronto, ON M4V 1E2

Published in the U.S. by
Kids Can Press Ltd.
2250 Military Road
Tonawanda, NY 14150

www.kidscanpress.com

Edited by Tara Walker
Designed by Stacie Bowes

Printed in Hong Kong, China, by Wing King Tong Company Limited

CM 02 0 9 8 7 6 5 4 3 2 1
CM PA 02 0 9 8 7 6 5 4 3 2 1

National Library of Canada Cataloguing in Publication Data

Jennings, Sharon
        Franklin and the magic show

(Kids Can Read)
The character Franklin was created by Paulette Bourgeois and Brenda Clark.

ISBN 1-55074-990-0 (bound)   ISBN 1-55074-992-7 (pbk.)

I. Jeffrey, Sean. II. Sinkner, Alice. III. Southern, Shelley. IV. Bourgeois, Paulette.
V. Clark, Brenda. VI. Title. VII. Series: Kids Can Read (Toronto, Ont.).

PS8569.E563F717 2002   jC813'.54   C2002-900063-7
PZ7.J429877frm 2002

Kids Can Press is a *l,©rus*™ Entertainment company

Franklin and the Magic Show

Kids Can Press

Franklin can tie his shoes.

Franklin can count by twos.

But Franklin cannot disappear.

This is a problem because

Franklin wants to be a magician.

One day, Franklin saw

a magic show.

Marten the Magnificent

did lots of tricks.

He turned a flower into a bird.

He made a chair rise up in the air.

He even made himself disappear.

"Wow!" said Franklin.

"I want to be a magician!"

Franklin ran home.

He found a hat

under his desk.

He found a cape

in his closet.

He found a magic wand

behind his toy box.

He found a book

of magic tricks on his shelf.

"Now I look like a magician,"

said Franklin.

"Now I can put on a magic show."

Franklin went to show his parents.

"I am Franklin the Fabulous,"

he told them.

"You look like a magician,"

said his mother.

"What tricks can you do?"

asked his father.

"I can disappear," said Franklin.

"That's a hard trick,"

said his father.

"Not for me," said Franklin.

Franklin went to find his friends.

"Is it Halloween?"

asked Bear.

"No," said Franklin.

"I am Franklin the Fabulous.

I am putting on a magic show.

You must pay one cookie to watch."

"I'll come," said Bear.

"I'll come," said Beaver.

"We'll all come,"

said everyone.

Franklin ran home to get ready.

Soon his friends came

with their cookies.

Franklin took a bow.

"I am Franklin the Fabulous,"

he said.

Then he waved his magic wand.

Everyone clapped.

"Now I will disappear,"

said Franklin.

"Ohhh!" said everyone.

Franklin got into a big box.

"Count to ten," he told his friends.

"Then open the box."

Franklin closed

the lid.

It was dark

inside the box.

"ONE! TWO! THREE!"

said Franklin's friends.

Franklin pushed

on the back

of the box.

"FOUR! FIVE! SIX!"

said Franklin's friends.

Franklin pushed
and pushed.

"SEVEN! EIGHT! NINE!"

said Franklin's friends.

Franklin could not
sneak out the
back of the box.
It was stuck.

"TEN!" said Franklin's friends.

They opened up the box.

"You did not disappear,"

said Beaver.

"I'm going home."

"Me too," said Fox.

"Me too," said Bear. "And I'm

taking my cookie."

"Me too," said everyone.

Franklin went to his room.

"I am not a magician,"

he told his mother.

"I am not Franklin the Fabulous,"

he told his father.

"I am just Franklin,

and I cannot disappear."

"That's a hard trick,"

said his father.

"I can show you an easy trick."

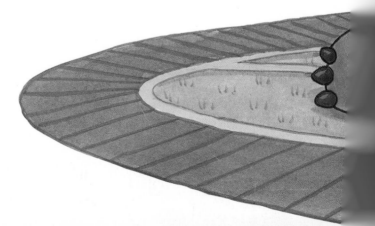

Franklin's father held a penny

in his left hand.

Then he closed both of his hands.

"Where's the penny?" he asked.

Franklin pointed to his left hand.

His father opened his right hand.

In it was the penny.

"Ta dah!" said Franklin's father.

"Wow!" said Franklin.

Franklin's father opened his left hand.

He had a penny in that hand, too.

"You have two pennies!"

cried Franklin.

"I tricked you," said his father.

"That was an easy trick,"

said Franklin.

"I know lots of easy tricks,"

said his father.

"Hmmm," said Franklin.

The next day,

Franklin got out his hat,

his cape and his magic wand.

He went to find his friends.

"I am Franklin the Fabulous,"

he said.

"I am putting on a magic show.

I will give you each a cookie

if you come."

"I'll come," said Bear.

"I'll come," said Beaver.

"We'll all come," said everyone.

Franklin the Fabulous

put on a very good magic show.

He did lots of easy tricks,

but he did not try to disappear.

Only one thing disappeared ...

... the cookies.